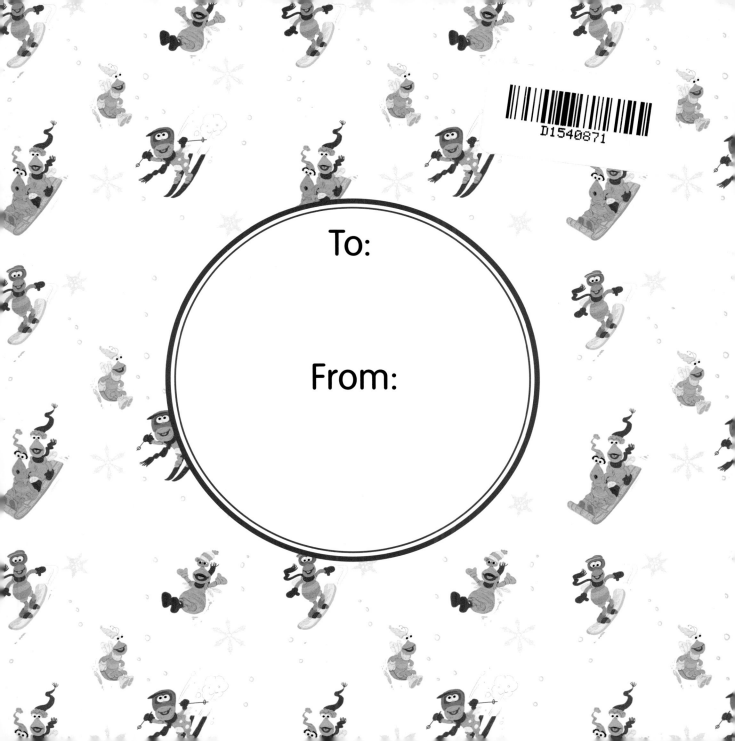

To:

From:

Cover and internal design © 2022 by Sourcebooks
Cover and internal illustrations © Sesame Workshop
Illustrations by Joe Mathieu

Sourcebooks and the colophon are registered trademarks of Sourcebooks.

Published by Sourcebooks Wonderland, an imprint of Sourcebooks Kids
P.O. Box 4410, Naperville, Illinois 60567-4410
(630) 961-3900
sourcebookskids.com

Source of Production: Wing King Tong Paper Products Co. Ltd., Shenzhen, Guangdong Province, China
Date of Production: April 2022
Run Number: 5025501

Printed and bound in China.
WKT 10 9 8 7 6 5 4 3 2 1

JoY to the WoRLD

words by Lillie ... ... Mathieu

sourcebooks
wonderland

Joy is being merry and bright and the feeling of cheer.

Joy is helping others with big things and small.

Joy is showing kindness and care to those in need.

Joy is spreading warm wishes to everyone you see, at home, at school, or in the neighborhood!

Joy is the traditions we look forward to each year.

Joy is making new ones too!

FUN RUN/WALK FOR CHARITY

JOY is snowflakes that sparkle as they fall.

Joy is laughter and fun that never ends.

JOY is making your favorite holiday treats.

JOY is sharing them with your neighbors.

Joy is giving—wrapping presents for those we love.

JOY is saying "thank you" and being grateful for the moments spent together.

Joy is bringing smiles to family and friends.

JOY is writing a letter to Santa who lives at the North Pole!

Joy is making memories with those who may be far away.

JOY is making decorations and putting them on your tree.

Joy is coloring Christmas cards and sending them to others.

Joy is reading a new story with someone special.

JOY is gathering together for milk and Christmas cookies.

JOY is singing carols all together.

Joy is the countdown to Christmas—only a few days away!

Joy is watching the twinkle of lights that shine bright.

JOY is putting out cookies and milk for Santa and his reindeer.

JOY is snuggling together with hearts full of love.

JOY is a Merry Christmas with peace, love, and joy to the world!

JOY TO THE WORLD

Share some holiday cheer!

During your countdown to Christmas, ask a grown-up to help you try some of the activities below with family and friends and spread joy at home and in your neighborhood!

1. Make a Christmas countdown chain with construction paper.

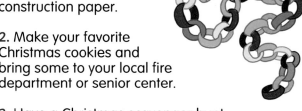

2. Make your favorite Christmas cookies and bring some to your local fire department or senior center.

3. Have a Christmas scavenger hunt.

4. Make hot cocoa and share with others.

5. Read a new story together.

6. Make care bags for those in need. These can include simple things like shelf-stable foods, toothbrushes, soap, and hand warmers.

7. Write a letter to Santa.

8. Draw pictures or take photographs to capture your memories for the Christmas season.

9. Make your own Christmas presents.

10. Practice saying "thank you" and write a thank you letter to your delivery driver, teacher, or garbage collector.

11. Pick a new Christmas tradition to start in your family.

12. Leave cookies and milk for Santa.

13. Make your own Christmas cards to send to family and friends.

14. Have a Christmas lights tour around the neighborhood.

15. Make dinner for a friend in need.

16. Attend your town's parade or Christmas events.

17. Deliver Christmas gifts to your neighbors.

18. Clean out your toy bin and donate to charity.

19. Contribute to a canned food drive.

20. Send a care package to a member of the military.

21. Offer to help decorate for the holidays at your local school or after-school center.

22. Sing Christmas carols to neighbors.

23. Take food and small toys to an animal shelter.

24. Make crafts to cheer up patients at a local children's hospital.

25. Make Christmas ornaments to decorate your tree.

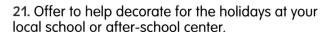